To all my favorite teachers (and the other ones too)—D.W.

To teachers everywhere who can do anything and everything
and to one special teacher at Grant Elementary—D. C.

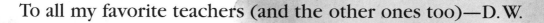
SIMON & SCHUSTER BOOKS FOR YOUNG READERS
An imprint of Simon & Schuster Children's Publishing Division
1230 Avenue of the Americas, New York, New York 10020
Text copyright © 2002 by Douglas Wood
Illustrations copyright © 2002 by Doug Cushman
SIMON & SCHUSTER BOOKS FOR YOUNG READERS is a trademark of Simon & Schuster.

Book design by Greg Stadnyk
The text of this book is set in Garamond.
The illustrations are rendered in pen and ink and watercolor.
Printed in the United States of America.
10 9 8 7 6 5 4 3 2 1

Library of Congress Cataloging-in-Publication Data
Wood, Douglas.
What teachers can't do / Douglas Wood ; pictures by Doug Cushman.—1st ed.
p. cm.
Summary: Details the many things that teachers cannot do, from buying their own apples to
going down the tube slide at recess.
ISBN 0-689-84644-4
[1. Teachers—Fiction.] I. Cushman, Doug, ill. II. Title.
PZ7.W847375 Who 2002
[E]—dc21
2001049904

What Teachers Can't Do

by Douglas Wood

pictures by Doug Cushman

Simon & Schuster Books for Young Readers

New York   London   Toronto   Sydney   Singapore

There are lots of things that regular people can do, but teachers can't.

Teachers can't ride skateboards or scooters to school.

They can never be tardy.

Teachers can't buy their own apples.

And they can't teach their best without flowers on their desk.

Teachers can spell "Mississippi" and "encyclopedia."

But they can't spell "CAT."

They can never quite remember what 2 + 2 is, either.

Teachers can't write on the chalkboard without squeaking.

They can't sit in the little chairs, even for story time.

And they can't use the hall pass to go to the bathroom.

Teachers can't cut to the front of the line.

Well . . . okay.

But they aren't allowed to trade desserts.

Teachers *may not* finger paint in their good clothes!

They can twirl but they can't jump.

Teachers can't cry if they skin *their* knees. Can they?

Sometimes teachers forget . . . no snoring during quiet time.

Teachers can't feed the salamander
or guinea pigs by themselves.

And sometimes they need help finding them!

Teachers can never run out of smiles.
Or smiley faces.

Teachers can't wait to come back to school tomorrow.

But first they really need some help cleaning the blackboard.

And they can't see out of the backs of their heads. Do you think?

Teachers can't go down the tube slide at recess. . . .

And the erasers!

No one knows why there are so many things teachers can't do.
Maybe because they're so busy doing the thing they do best of all.

Teaching you.